A
FIC
KID

3276

FIRST UNITED METHODIST CHURCH
So. Winooski Ave. at Buell St.
Office: 21 Buell St.
Burlington, Vermont 05401

DEMCO

BUILDING FRIENDS

BUILDING FRIENDS

Written by
RONALD KIDD

Illustrated by
CORNELIUS VAN WRIGHT & YING-HWA HU

A Habitat for Humanity Book

HABITAT FOR HUMANITY INTERNATIONAL
Americus, Georgia

To Tony, Cathy, Kelsey, and Jason
—R.K.

To my father Edward, the carpenter
—C.V.W.

Published by Habitat for Humanity International
121 Habitat Street
Americus, Georgia 31709-3498
1-800-422-4828

Millard Fuller	*President and Founder*
Joy Highnote	*Director, Product Development*
Joseph Matthews	*Director, Communication Services*

Edited, designed, and manufactured by
The Children's Marketplace
A division of Southwestern/Great American, Inc.
2451 Atrium Way, Nashville, Tennessee 37214
1-800-358-0560

Dave Kempf	*Vice President, Executive Editor*
Mary Cummings	*Managing Editor*
Ronald Kidd	*Project Editor*
Bruce Gore	*Book Design*

For we are God's fellow workers;
you are God's field, you are God's building.

1 Corinthians 3:9

Rosa sat in her treehouse, smiling.

The treehouse was Rosa's favorite place. Her mother and father had built it for her when they moved to their new neighborhood, to make her feel at home.

Rosa loved sitting high above the ground, safe among the branches, watching the world go by.

One Saturday morning, Rosa saw a boy ride his bike onto the empty lot next door. He parked the bike and sat down in the lot, gazing out across the wildflowers and weeds.

Rosa, curious, climbed down from the tree and walked over to where the boy sat.

"What are you doing?" asked Rosa
The boy said, "Just enjoying the view."
Rosa told him about her treehouse
and invited him to see it. The boy, whose
name was Matthew, thanked her but said
he should be getting home. He promised
to ask his parents if he could return the
next week.

After church on Sunday, Rosa's
mother and father had some news.

"We learned about a group called
Habitat for Humanity," said Rosa's mother.
"Habitat builds houses for working families
who need a decent place to live. All the
builders are volunteers. That means they
don't do it for money. They do it because
they want to help."

Rosa's father said, "We've decided to
volunteer for Habitat and help build a
brand-new house."

"Can I help?" asked Rosa.

"I'm afraid not," said her father. "For safety reasons, only grownups are allowed."

Her mother said, "But you can still feel like part of the project, because the house will be right next door. You can watch the whole thing from your treehouse!"

Saturday was a big day for Rosa. The volunteers started work on the Habitat house, and her new friend Matthew came to play. Rosa and Matthew spent the day in the treehouse, talking and watching the Habitat workers.

Matthew came back the next week, but this time he brought a toolbox with him.

"I like building things, too," said Matthew. "If you want, we could work on your treehouse together." Rosa happily agreed, and the two of them got started.

Week by week, as the children fixed up Rosa's treehouse, the Habitat house took shape. They watched each step from their perch in the tree, waving to Rosa's parents and the other volunteers.

First the workers laid the foundation, so the house would rest on a solid base.

Next the workers built the walls and
roof, with windows and doors to let in
the sun.

Finally the house was finished and painted. It was completed the same day Rosa and Matthew did the last of their work on the treehouse.

At dinner that night, Rosa's father told her the Habitat house would be dedicated on Saturday. There would be a short service, and then the new family would move in.

Rosa's mother was still excited about her work on the house. She said, "One of the best things about it was meeting people. I think building things together is a good way to make friends."

Thinking of Matthew, Rosa agreed.

A few days later, Rosa called Matthew to see if he could come play on Saturday. "I can't play this week," he said, "but I'll be seeing you soon."

FIRST UNITED METHODIST CHURCH
So. Winooski Ave. at Buell St.
Office: 21 Buell St.
Burlington, Vermont 05401

At the dedication on Saturday, Rosa stood with her parents, listening to the speakers. The last speaker presented a set of keys to the family who would be living there. Rosa stood on tiptoe to see her new neighbors. There was a mother, a father, and a little boy.

The boy was Matthew.

When Matthew introduced Rosa to his parents, she recognized them as two of the workers who had built the house.

"Why didn't you tell me you'd be living here?" Rosa asked Matthew.

"I was too shy at first," he said. "Then I decided to make it a surprise."

Matthew proudly led Rosa into his new house. It was still empty, but the morning sun made it feel warm and welcoming.

Then Matthew took her to his room. He sat in the middle of the floor, gazed out the window, and grinned, just as he had done that first day in the empty lot.

Rosa sat down beside him to see what he was looking at. There, framed in the window, was Rosa's treehouse.

"I liked the view before," said Matthew. "But now it's even better."

Rosa smiled and took his hand. She said, "Everything looks better when you have a friend."

RONALD KIDD is the author of thirty books for young audiences and five plays. He received the Children's Choice Award and was nominated for the Edgar Allan Poe Award. Two of his plays were selected for development at the Eugene O'Neill Theater Center's National Playwrights Conference. He lives with his wife in Nashville, Tennessee.

CORNELIUS VAN WRIGHT and YING-HWA HU are a husband and wife team who have been working together since 1989. Cornelius studied at the School of Art and Design and the School of Visual Arts in New York. Ying-Hwa studied at Shi Chen College in Taiwan and St. Cloud State University. Their picture book *Zora Hurston and the Chinaberry Tree* was a 1996 Reading Rainbow selection. The couple live in New York City with their daughter and son.

Habitat for Humanity International
121 Habitat Street
Americus, Georgia 31709-3498

For more information, please call
1-800-HABITAT